STADIUM SCHOOL

WHERE FOOTBALLING DREAMS COME TRUE

Long
Shot

Jefferies & Goffe

A & C Black • London

*To Paul, for getting me into
football in the first place. SG*

First published 2008 by
A & C Black Publishers Ltd
38 Soho Square, London, W1D 3HB

www.acblack.com

Text copyright © 2008 C. Jefferies and S. Goffe

ISBN 978-1-4081-0080-6

A CIP catalogue for this book is available from the British Library.

This book is produced using paper that is made from wood
grown in managed, sustainable forests. It is natural, renewable and
recyclable. The logging and manufacturing processes conform
to the environmental regulations of the country of origin.

Printed and bound in Great Britain by CPI Cox & Wyman, Reading, RG1 8EX

Long
Shot

Contents

Map of S

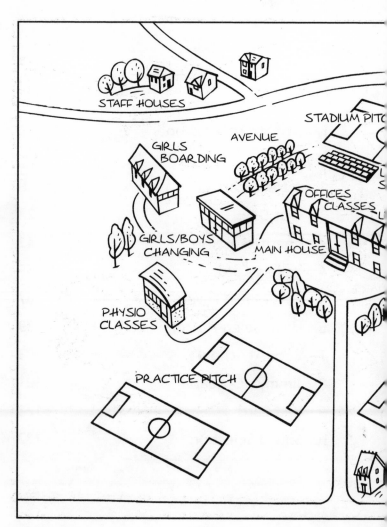

STAFF HOUSES

AVENUE

STADIUM PITCH

GIRLS BOARDING

OFFICES CLASSES

GIRLS/BOYS CHANGING

MAIN HOUSE

PHYSIO CLASSES

PRACTICE PITCH

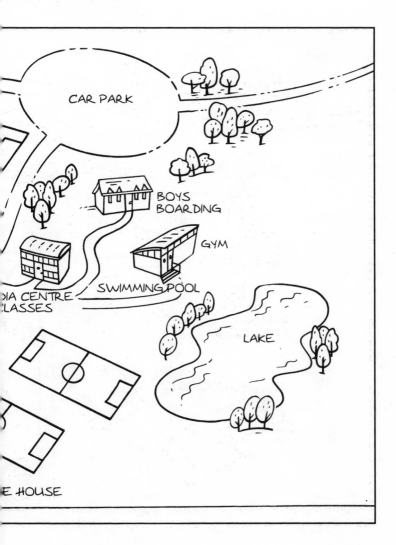

CAR PARK

BOYS BOARDING

GYM

MEDIA CENTRE
CLASSES

SWIMMING POOL

LAKE

E HOUSE

1. A New Start

Roddy Jones tried to get closer, so he could read the notice board in the hall. But it was impossible. There was such a crush of people. It was going to be odd, not being top dog any more. At his last school, people would have made way for him. He'd had loads of respect there because he was the best footballer they'd ever had. But Stadium School was a boarding school for talented young footballers, all wanting to make it to the top. He'd have to do something very special to stand out now.

"Roddy?"

Someone tapped him on the shoulder and he turned round.

Long Shot

"Geno!" A broad grin spread across his face. "You got in! That's fantastic!"

Geno grinned back. "Yeah. You, too."

Dark-haired Geno was small and wiry like Roddy, and a great striker. They'd met at the trial in the summer, and hit it off immediately. Roddy had been totally blown away to discover that Geno's dad was the great Luca Perotti, the famous Italian international.

"This is *so* cool," said Roddy, abandoning his attempt to get to the notice board. "Have you been here long?"

"Quite a while," said Geno. "I already knew you'd got in because I saw your name on the board. *And*," he added. "Guess what? We're both in Charlton House!"

"Wow!" said Roddy. "That's great."

Information about the four houses had been sent in the welcome pack after Roddy had found out he'd won his place at the

A New Start

school. The houses would all play matches against each other over the course of the year, with the overall winner claiming the House Cup.

Roddy was thrilled to find that they'd be playing in the same team. We'll annihilate the opposition!" he bragged.

Geno laughed. "Hopefully," he said. "This is Jimmy Piper," he added, pointing to the well-built, fair-haired boy standing next to him. "He's in Charlton, too. He plays centre back."

"Hi," said Jimmy. "What position do you play?"

"Midfield," said Roddy, pleased to meet another friendly face in this room full of strangers.

"Jimmy and I are sharing," Geno told Roddy. "Have you met any of your roommates yet?"

Long Shot

"No one was there when I dumped my stuff," said Roddy. "So I came straight over here to see what was happening."

"Not a lot until tea," said Geno. "And I've already done my unpacking."

"Yeah. Your mate's really well organised," laughed Jimmy. "I just left my bag on the bed."

Roddy smiled. "Me, too," he admitted. "Hey, we could go back to the boarding house and check out the common room until tea, if you like."

Both Geno and Jimmy nodded, but someone else had just caught Roddy's eye. "Hang on a minute," he said, and hurried over to a girl with long, blonde hair, who had just come into the hall with two other girls.

"Hello, Keira," said Roddy. He was delighted that Keira Sanders had got a place at the school. She was a midfielder, too, and really bubbly and enthusiastic.

A New Start

"Roddy! It's wonderful to see you," she said. "I hoped you'd get in."

"Same here." Roddy hesitated, unsure how to continue the conversation, after having been so eager to start it. "I'm in Charlton," he said awkwardly. "How about you?"

"I'm in Charlton, too!" Keira whooped. "How can we lose? Isn't this all..." She gestured around the room full of students. "Just brilliant!"

For a moment they both stood there, overflowing with disbelief and excitement. They exchanged grins, and then Roddy cleared his throat. "Well ... er ... I suppose I'd better go. I'm with Geno. But I just wanted to say hi. See you at tea maybe?"

"Sure." Keira flashed him another smile. "I've got to find my room and dump my bags, but I wouldn't miss tea for *anything*."

Roddy, Geno and Jimmy headed outside

Long Shot

and made their way along a path towards the boarding house. They passed a bunch of boys heading a ball to each other in the autumn sunshine.

"What number is your room?" asked Roddy.

"Four," said Geno.

Roddy stopped in his tracks. "*Four*?"

Jimmy gave him an odd look. "What's wrong with that?" he asked.

"Nothing's *wrong* with it," said Roddy. "Only … that's *my* room as well."

"Awesome," said Geno. "Looks like we'll be sharing!"

Roddy laughed. "I can't believe it … I wonder who the fourth person will be?"

"Let's just hope they don't snore," said Jimmy.

Roddy laughed again. "Do you play table football?" he asked Jimmy, as they arrived at the boarding house.

A New Start

"Of course," said Jimmy. "And I bet I could beat you, too."

"Bet you couldn't," said Roddy.

"Game on!" said Geno.

There were a few other boys in the common room, and more new people were arriving all the time. The three roommates went over to the table football, but as Jimmy was about to pick up the ball, another boy barged in and grabbed it.

"Oi!" said Jimmy. "We were just going to play."

"Too late," said the boy unpleasantly. "I got here first."

Roddy's heart sank. He was almost certain that the boy was a midfielder called Jack. At the trial, Roddy had overheard someone describe him as a thug. He hoped it wasn't true, but this wasn't a very good start.

"Who were you going to play with?"

Long Shot

he asked.

Jack looked at Roddy. "I'll take *you* on," he said aggressively.

Jimmy rolled his eyes. "He doesn't even have anyone to *play* with," he muttered. "What a sad act!"

Jack gave Jimmy a murderous look and Roddy butted in to stop the bad atmosphere turning into a fight.

"I'll play you next, if you like," he said to Jack. "As soon as Jimmy and I have had our go."

Jack glared at Roddy, and Roddy shrugged.

"*You* then," Jack said, turning to Geno.

Geno shook his head. "No, thanks," he said. "I'm just watching."

Jack shoved the ball into his jeans pocket and started to walk away. "OK, losers," he sneered. "No one plays."

Roddy and Jimmy were furious. "Give us the ball back," they demanded.

A New Start

"Leave it!" Geno advised. "He's not worth it."

But Jimmy wasn't listening. He was about to make a grab for Jack, when a member of staff arrived.

"Jack! What are you doing?" It was the boarding-house master, Mr Clutterbuck.

Jack shrugged. "Nothing. Just having a bit of a laugh."

"We were trying to play table football and he nicked the ball," protested Jimmy.

Jack looked daggers at Jimmy. "Can't you take a joke?" he sneered.

Mr Clutterbuck looked at each of the boys in turn. "Let's see if you can get on, shall we?" he suggested. He looked at Jack again, who reached reluctantly into his pocket and produced the ball.

"There you go," he said, and tossed it vaguely in Jimmy's direction. It fell some

Long Shot

distance from Jimmy's outstretched hand, and rolled under the pool table.

Geno retrieved it and put it back.

"Now listen," said Mr Clutterbuck, giving Jack a hard look. "You're all new to Stadium School, and you're here because you're talented, determined and very competitive on the football field. Don't let that competitive spirit turn into unfriendliness or bullying off the pitch now, please."

The three friends waited until Jack had wandered over to the TV and switched it on.

"I don't think much of him," muttered Roddy.

"He was in our team for the trial," said Jimmy. "I wouldn't want to play against him. He's good, but he tackled really aggressively."

"Maybe he'll settle down after a day or two," said Geno. "He's probably just stressed about not knowing anyone."

A New Start

"Maybe," said Roddy doubtfully. "Is he in Charlton with us?"

Geno shook his head. "I don't think so," he said. "I can't remember seeing his name on our house list."

Mr Clutterbuck was speaking again, but this time to the whole room. "Don't forget, tea is in the main house at five o'clock," he said.

"When's our first training session?" asked someone near to Roddy.

"Tomorrow morning," said Mr Clutterbuck. "And every morning after that, except Sundays." He smiled as a ragged cheer went up. "There should be calendars on your beds," he went on. "They have holiday dates and match fixtures inside, so don't lose them. And I've got timetables here. You lot can come and get them now, if you like."

The boys hurried forward to collect the timetables, and Jack made a point of pushing

Long Shot

in front of Jimmy, who winced.

"That idiot stamped on my foot!" Jimmy told his roommates as soon as Jack was out of the way.

"He did it deliberately," said Roddy. "I saw him."

"Don't worry, I'm not scared of Jack," laughed Jimmy, rubbing his bruised foot.

"If he annoys you again, I'll help you sort him out," said Roddy. "We can't have him injuring one of our defenders!"

"Thanks, mate," said Jimmy appreciatively.

"But now I really ought to go and put my stuff away," said Roddy. "Are you staying here?"

"Nah," said Jimmy. "I ought to unpack as well, I suppose. What are you going to do, Geno?"

"I'll come with you," said Geno. "Then we can all go to tea together."

A New Start

The boys trooped back to their room. It had been fairly tidy when they left, but now it looked as if a tornado had swept through it.

In the middle of the mess stood an extremely tall boy with a very serious expression on his face. As soon as he noticed the new arrivals, he dropped the shirt he'd just taken out of a large suitcase.

"Hello," he said in a deep voice. "I am Marek Dvorski, the best young striker in Poland. Am I sharing a room with you?"

"Er ... yes," said Roddy after a moment. He took in the boy's height, and impressive untidiness. "I suppose you are."

2. First Day

Marek looked rather forbidding at first, but Roddy soon realised that although he was serious, he was also very friendly.

By the time Marek had told them all about his delayed flight from Poland, his family and his football, they were all getting along just fine. And he was as impressed as Roddy to be sharing a room with Luca Perotti's son.

"I want to play for my country like Perotti did for his," he announced.

Everyone shared that footballing ambition and for a moment they were all quiet as they studied the poster of Italia '90 that Geno had put up over his bed. Then Roddy took charge. "I'm starving," he said. "Let's go and get tea."

First Day

"Good idea!" said Geno.

Keira was already at a table with a few girls when Roddy and his friends arrived. They went to the servery and loaded their trays with food.

"Hi," said Keira, when they went across to her table. "Come and join us. There's plenty of room. Did you know that Simon didn't get in, or Polly, the girl I was most friendly with?" she went on, as Roddy and the others sat down. "It's a shame, isn't it?"

Roddy nodded. "But *we* got in," he said with a broad grin. "By the way, this is Jimmy and Marek. "We're all sharing a room, along with Geno."

"I've got twins in my room," said Keira, indicating two identical girls with black hair tightly plaited into cornrows. "Meet demon wingers, Eboni and Ashanti. If you can tell them apart, you're better than me!"

The twins grinned at Roddy. "Hi!" said

Long Shot

Eboni. "We've already heard all about you. Don't you play in midfield, like Keira?"

"Sure do," Roddy told her. Then he pointed at his roommates. "Back, striker, and striker," he explained.

"Jess over there is another back," said the Ashanti, pointing to a blonde girl, who was carrying her tray to a table.

"Which house are you in?" asked Keira

"We're all in Charlton," said Geno.

"Great!" said Keira. "Let's make Charlton a force to be reckoned with." She was looking very confident. "Wouldn't it be brilliant if we could carry off the House Cup?"

"You bet!" agreed Ashanti.

"And there's a prize for each year as well," added Roddy, not to be outdone. "We might win that. We've got to be the best house team ever!"

"Hey, Roddy, you'd make a good captain

First Day

with talk like that," said Geno.

Roddy felt pleased. It would be great if he did make captain, just like in his old school.

But Eboni had other ideas. "I think Keira would make a good captain, too," she said.

Roddy and Keira looked at each other warily.

"Well," said Keira, "it doesn't matter who's captain, as long as they keep us on the ball!"

"Quite right," agreed Roddy, wishing he'd said it first.

He tried to come up with another upbeat remark, but the girls had already finished their tea, and were clattering the dirty dishes onto their trays.

"We're back off to our room now," said Keira. "See you tomorrow at practice, yeah?"

"Yeah," said Roddy munching his way through a large slice of pizza. "See you tomorrow."

Long Shot

After they'd finished eating, the boys returned to their cluttered room.

"Are you always this untidy?" Roddy asked with a grin, wading through a heap of Marek's clothes.

Marek shrugged. "I am a footballer," he said, as if that explained everything.

When Mr Clutterbuck came in to tell them to go to bed, he was horrified. "Good grief!" he said. "Get all this put away."

"Good grief!" echoed Marek, once the housemaster had gone. But he picked up most of the clothes, and shoved them into a cupboard. He closed his empty case and stowed it on top of the wardrobe.

"You ought to be a goalie with your height," said Jimmy admiringly.

But Marek didn't take it as a compliment. "No!" he said fiercely. "I told you before. I am a striker. The best striker in Poland one day!"

First Day

He glared at Jimmy, and Jimmy held up his hands in defence.

"OK!" he agreed. "Don't lose your rag. You're going to be a stormin' striker for Poland. I understand."

"Yes," said Marek, and he smiled.

Just before they got into bed, Roddy noticed Jimmy pull an old sock furtively out of his drawer and put it under his pillow. It was on the tip of Roddy's tongue to ask what he was doing, but the moment didn't seem right.

He had never shared a room before, and he supposed that everyone must have different habits. Geno had his poster and Marek had a small Polish flag draped over the end of his bed. Roddy had a Welsh flag, as well as a photograph of himself collecting a trophy at primary school. He was going to keep it in his drawer, but then he decided to put it on top of his bedside table. It would remind him that

Long Shot

winning was what it was all about. And if having an old sock under his pillow helped Jimmy in some way, well it was really none of Roddy's business.

There was an early start in the morning. Students had to fit in a full day of classes as well as all the extra football training that came with being at Stadium School. Roddy dragged himself out of bed with the others. He was so keen to get on with his training, he didn't mind losing a bit of sleep, even if he did feel a bit bleary eyed. He couldn't wait to find out what training was going to be like, though he was willing to bet that it would be a lot more serious than at his old school. But he prided himself in being pretty fit, and was sure he'd be able to cope.

The four friends pulled on their new, dark-green tracksuits, and headed across to the

First Day

main building for breakfast. It was still quite misty, but it looked as if the sun was going to soon break through.

"Hi, Roddy!" said Keira, who was already queuing up at the hatch.

"Hello," said Roddy, still half-asleep. "I can't remember the last time I got up this early."

"It's a pity we can't start training an hour later," put in Jimmy.

Keira frowned. "Aren't you itching to get out onto the field?" she asked.

"Well, I am, yes," said Jimmy. "That's true. I'm just not very good at getting up in the morning."

"You'll get used to it," she laughed.

As soon as breakfast was over, the students went back to their houses for registration. Mr Clutterbuck handed out timetables to the boys who hadn't been given them the night before. And then half an hour after they had

Long Shot

eaten, everyone was out on the training pitches, peeling off their tracksuits, and all the new students were gathered together in front of the head junior coach, Mr Jenkins.

Mr Jenkins had spotted Roddy at a football summer school in the holidays, and Roddy liked him a lot.

"It's good to see you all again," said Mr Jenkins. "I'll be your coach for the next three years. Sometimes my colleagues will work with you, but everything that happens in training comes back to me. Now, these morning sessions are short, so we'll mainly be concentrating on fitness. We'll do the more technical training after lessons. Let's start with some laps of the pitch, to see what sort of shape you're in. Follow my lead!"

And with that, he set off at a steady jog along the touchline, with the group strung out behind him. Every now and then, he would turn and run backwards for a few seconds to see how they were coping with his pace. Soon, they settled into a routine of jogging the lengths, and either sprinting or sidestepping the widths of the pitch.

Mr Jenkins threw in other wrinkles, too, like high knees, or skipping, then he had them all jogging on the spot. Roddy was coping extremely well with the workout, but he was panting hard.

"All right, we'll just do one final thing, as I can see some of you are getting tired. A straight sprint to the other end of the pitch, and don't worry about staying behind me. I want to see who's got anything left in the tank to run with. Three ... two ... one..."

The line of 50 students and their coach all charged headlong down the pitch, Mr Jenkins surprised everyone by pulling ahead, just before the halfway line.

Long Shot

"Come on! Can't any of you run faster than an old man?" he shouted, as he overtook them.

The squad redoubled their efforts, and by the time they reached the other end of the pitch, a few students, including Roddy and Keira, had caught up with and overtaken the agile coach.

Once he'd got his breath back, Mr Jenkins congratulated them all on a good first session. Everyone who had beaten him in the sprint was given five points for their house, then they all went off to get showered and changed before their first lesson.

"We're the first in our house to win points," Keira said to Roddy when they met up again after their showers. "Go us!"

Roddy grinned. Keira was right. It *did* feel good.

The Stadium School teachers were pretty good

at making even ordinary lessons interesting. Roddy particularly enjoyed English because they began reading a story about football, which he thought was great.

The morning passed quickly, and by lunchtime, Roddy was starving. He couldn't fault the chicken pie that was served, and there was plenty of it.

"It seems ages since the trial," he said between mouthfuls.

"I know," agreed Keira, who was sitting at their table again. "We've hardly been here a day and already I feel really settled. Do you remember that weird tree tunnel over by the old stadium seats?"

"I thought the trees sounded as if they were whispering!" said Roddy. "That whole set-up was crazy, wasn't it?"

"What trees?" asked Marek. "What set-up?"

Long Shot

"Didn't you get to see them on the guided tour?" asked Keira. "We were all taken round in groups."

Marek nodded. "No," he said. "My group was the last and there wasn't much time, so we didn't get there."

"Well, did you know that this school was built on the site of an old football stadium?" said Roddy.

"Of course," said Marek in a dignified voice. "And I know it was the first stadium that the famous Jon Masters played in."

"OK," said Roddy. "Well, he wanted to preserve the tunnel that goes from the dressing rooms to the pitch, but it burnt down."

"So he planted an avenue of trees there instead," put in Keira. "And when you play on the Stadium pitch, you have to walk down this sort of tree tunnel."

First Day

"And there's a group of original seats at the end," said Geno, "that are supposed to be lucky."

"Why don't we take Marek there?" suggested Roddy. "We've got time before afternoon lessons start."

"I would like that," said Marek looking pleased.

"OK, let's go!" said Keira, getting up.

"I'm not sure..." started Jimmy, but Geno interrupted him.

"If we hurry, we'll have time to take him all the way down the tunnel," he said. "You have to see the pitch, Marek. It's fantastic. Premier League standard. It's only used for important matches, and for the finals of the House Cup."

They all set off, and in a few minutes reached the changing rooms.

"I don't see any tree tunnel around here," said Marek, looking about him.

Long Shot

"It's at the back," said Roddy, leading the way.

Sure enough, behind the changing rooms, there was a double row of young trees with a path between them.

"It's fantastic!" said Marek enthusiastically. "And how clever, to grow the trees like this to make a tunnel."

"Wait until you see the seats," said Geno. "It looks so strange, doesn't it, having a bunch of stadium seats without the stadium."

Jimmy shrugged. He seemed a bit uneasy.

"On the day of the trial, I almost sat in the one that's all charred from the fire," said Roddy. "But no one is allowed to sit in it because it was Jon Masters's seat when he came here as a child."

Keira laughed. "There's a whole mythology about the place, isn't there," she said. "Did they tell you there was supposed to be a

First Day

ghost here? The girl who showed our group round said that someone died in the old stadium fire, and their ghost haunts this tree tunnel leading to the football field, and the seats as well."

"I don't believe that!" laughed Roddy. "Our guide said that the old stadium was burnt down after it had been abandoned. There wasn't anyone there to get hurt in the fire."

"There might have been," said Jimmy. "It *is* spooky here."

"You don't believe in ghosts, do you, Jimmy?" Roddy grinned at his roommate, but his smile faded as he realised Jimmy was serious. "Come on, people are always making up spooky stories. It doesn't mean they're true. Besides, who could believe in ghosts on a day like today?"

He was right. The sun was shining, and everything looked quite harmless, but as they

Long Shot

got further into the tree tunnel, the light changed to a kind of green dusk, and the rustling leaves *did* sound uncannily like people whispering. The temperature had dropped a bit, too. It would be easy to imagine all kinds of things going on here.

"I think I'll wait for you," said Jimmy, backing away to the start of the tunnel again.

"Once we're in the first team, and allowed to walk down here onto the Stadium pitch, you won't be thinking of ghosts!" said Geno.

"Let him go," said Roddy quietly, as Jimmy hurried away. "I think he's quite superstitious."

At the far end of the tunnel, they emerged once again into sunlight. The pitch lay straight ahead, but Keira stopped Marek from walking onto it. "It's out of bounds," she warned. "We have to earn the right to play on it – which means we need to get into the first team for our year. I can't wait!"

First Day

Marek had a look at the preserved seats – the only ones that were left from the original stand. It was just a couple of rows of wooden seats. Most of them were brightly painted in the blue-and-green Stadium School colours, but one stood out amongst them – it was charred black, and had obviously been left that way since the fire.

"Don't sit down!" shouted Geno.

"Why not?" said Marek, who was just about to sit on one of the painted seats. "I'm not stupid; I wasn't going to sit in Jon Masters's seat."

"But the painted ones are only for the winners of the house competition," explained Roddy. "The rest of us have to stand on the touchline to watch big matches."

"We will be sitting there at the end of the year," predicted Marek in his serious voice.

"Let's hope so," said Roddy. "Come on.

Long Shot

We'd better go back and find Jimmy. It's almost time for our next class."

At the end of the afternoon, there was another training session. This time, Mr Jenkins announced that they would play a match. The students in Banks House would play against Moore, while Charlton took on Stiles.

Roddy had thought he was pretty fit, but he struggled to keep up with several of the group, including Keira. She was seriously good, and Roddy realised that if he wanted to get into the first team he'd need to work hard, and harder still if he was going to make it as captain.

Charlton took an early lead, but Roddy felt he was struggling to make an impression on the game, while Keira was drawing Mr Jenkins' most vocal praise.

Jones is looking a little subdued today, and

First Day

definitely not having a good game by his own high standards. Luckily for Charlton House, the slack is being taken up by his midfield partner, Sanders. She is causing the Stiles defence all sorts of problems with her spectacular runs and searching passes. The ball comes to Jones now, but he plays the simple pass to Sanders, who goes off on another run. Jones follows the play up the pitch, but is not involved as Sanders threads the ball expertly between the central defenders to play in Dvorski, who almost bursts the net with a powerful strike. The outcome of this match is put beyond doubt, and the coach calls time on this disappointing outing for Jones, who makes way for a substitute. He's going to have to play a lot better than this to catch the eye of his new manager.

As both teams trooped off the pitch, Mr Jenkins had words of encouragement for every player, but Roddy was sure that he

Long Shot

singled Keira out for special praise. A token
few words was not enough for him. He told
himself that he would do better the next day.
Keira was a seriously good player, and he was
determined to be every bit as good as she was.

3. Charlton House

At breakfast the next morning, Roddy and his friends were chatting quietly when a senior boy stood up and banged the table to get attention.

"House meetings for first years will take place straight after tea today," he announced. "Stiles will squeeze into the library, Charlton will be in the hall, Banks at the gym, and as last year's winning team, Moore gets to stay in the dining room."

There was an even greater buzz of chatter as the boy sat down again, but it was nearly time to get ready for training, so they quickly finished their breakfast and, after registration, headed over to the changing rooms.

Long Shot

As before, Mr Jenkins concentrated on building up their physical strength.

"It doesn't matter how good you are," he said. "If you can't run for the last ten minutes of a game, you'll concede goals against teams who can. It's the score at the end of a match that's important, not half-time. So, three laps of the pitch while I set up some sprint exercises for you. Get going, everyone!"

After training, it was maths, one of Roddy's least favourite lessons. Mr Henderson tried to make it more interesting with football-related questions, but it was difficult to make percentages fun. Roddy decided that if he made it big, he would have an agent to work out the fine details of his contract. *He* would concentrate on playing great football.

Before lunch, Mr Jenkins gave a lesson on tactics. Roddy had been looking forward to it, and hurried to get a good seat in the swanky media centre. The junior coach spent most of the time introducing everyone to the different programmes they could use to demonstrate tactics. There was one similar to the kind that pundits used on TV to highlight important players in the playbacks. Another programme allowed you to move virtual players around and organise them to play in different ways.

"A lot of people are still using boards with magnets to do this kind of thing," said Mr Jenkins. "But at Stadium School we can use the latest technology to make it much more realistic. For instance, when we show a corner-taking routine, we can factor in things like the heights of players, and then play the set piece through to see how it works."

He loaded up a plan that the senior teams used, and ran it through to show them. The figures on the screen were obviously not real

Long Shot

players, but the way they moved was very convincing. The first time Mr Jenkins ran the simulation, a defender managed to clear the ball, but the second time, it rocketed into the back of the net, getting a few cheers from the class. Roddy found it fascinating, and for the rest of the day his head was filled with formations and set pieces.

Later, when it was time for the house meeting, Roddy and his friends hurried over to the hall.

A senior boy took charge. "I'm David Leval," he said. "I'm in my final year at Stadium School, and I was voted captain of Charlton last term. It's my job to tell the new students what our house is all about."

"Hopefully winning!" Keira whispered to Roddy.

"A major part of the house competition is the football," David continued, after giving

Keira a sharp look. "But it's not all just about winning. Although the most points are given for a win, other points are given for goals scored and clean sheets, and they're taken off for red and yellow cards. Charlton are known for our attacking approach on the pitch, and we always try to rack up as many bonus points for goals as we can."

Roddy smiled to himself, anticipating all the great attacking play he would be doing. He imagined himself scoring shedloads of goals.

"Don't forget," David continued. "The teachers don't let us get away with shoddy academic work, and if they think we're slacking, they're quite capable of giving us a yellow, or even a red, card for that. A yellow card means minus ten points and a red is minus 25. And, just like in a match, a red card means you miss the next house match, so we want you to avoid cards as much as possible."

Long Shot

"But what if you're just not very good at a subject?" asked Roddy. "It seems a bit harsh."

"Good point," said David. "Of course we'll be thrilled if you're an academic whiz; the bonus points can help a lot. But the red and yellow cards are used to punish lack of effort. As long as you're trying, the teachers will be happy enough. What they don't want is for us to be so focused on football that we forget about everything else."

"Our housemaster said we could be docked points for bad behaviour, too," said a boy to Roddy's left.

David nodded. "That's right," he said. "Bad behaviour can also get a red or yellow card. So you see, it's not just winning our house matches that's important, we have to make sure we don't lose unnecessary points and, if possible, we need to win a few, too.

"Good leadership gets points, and helpful

behaviour. You don't need to suck up to the teachers," he said hastily, as several groans went up. "Just concentrate on not being total idiots."

"Make sure you don't prat about then, Roddy," said Keira with a cheeky grin.

David glared at Keira's interruption. "It doesn't matter so much now," he said. "But talking in lessons can easily lose you points, and if you keep it up, you might receive a yellow card."

Keira blushed.

"OK," David went on. "We'll have a run out of you first years before tea tomorrow. We want to see what we've got in the way of talent in our new players. We were so close to winning the House Cup last year; you lot could make all the difference.

"Of course, as juniors you play mixed football. The seniors play single-sex games,

Long Shot

so we don't have so many people to choose from. But it's the same for every house, and all the Charlton teams do pretty well, right the way up through the school. Don't forget, there is a cup for each year, too – an extra incentive to do your best in all the matches."

Roddy felt really excited. He wanted to talk about it with his friends. But David was speaking again.

"The first house matches will be later in the week," he said. "So you'll be able to come and cheer our teams on. Hopefully we will inspire you! First years don't start matches until the week before half term, to give you time to bond as a team both on and off the pitch. As you know, everyone plays six games a term, apart from the first years, who only have three in their first term."

Roddy and Geno grinned at each other.

"Right," said David. "That's about it. Don't

forget to come along to practice straight after lessons tomorrow. We'll meet on the field nearest the changing rooms. I'll be there and so will Sam." He nodded towards a friendly looking girl with short, brown hair. "Sam will be the Charlton first years' coach."

Sam gave them a beaming smile.

"See you tomorrow, then," said David.

"See you tomorrow," added Sam. "Don't be late!"

Back at the boarding house, Roddy struggled a bit with his maths homework, and was one of the last to finish. Geno waited for him, then they went back to their bedroom to see what the others were up to.

When they got there, the room was in chaos. But this time it was Jimmy throwing clothes around, while Marek was sitting on his bed in silence.

Long Shot

"What's going on?" asked Roddy.

"Jimmy has lost something," said Marek.

"Well, what is it?" said Geno. "We'll help you look."

Jimmy stopped scrabbling about under his bed and stood up. He looked both embarrassed and very anxious.

"He wouldn't tell me!" said Marek.

"I just... Sorry." Jimmy looked at Marek, and Marek shrugged. "Promise you won't laugh?"

"Of course we won't laugh," said Roddy.

"It's my sock," said Jimmy.

"Your sock?" said Marek.

"Do you only have one?" said Geno.

"No, of course not," Jimmy said. "But this is a special sock."

"What's special about it?" asked Geno.

Jimmy bit his lip. "It's lucky," he said.

Geno started to laugh and then stopped.

Jimmy glared at him. "It is," he insisted. "I wore it when I was picked for the team at my old school, and every time I've worn it since, something good happens. I've grown out of it now, but I still need it."

Roddy stared at him. He'd had Jimmy down as being a bit superstitious since his reaction to the tree tunnel and the ghost story. "Is it the sock you usually keep under your pillow?" he asked.

Jimmy looked even more embarrassed. "I didn't think anyone knew," he said miserably. "I put it there to keep it safe. But now it's gone, and all my luck is going to run out. I won't get into the first team, *or* do well for Charlton House. I'll probably get loads of red cards and end up being expelled!"

"Don't be so ridiculous," said Marek.

Jimmy looked as if he wanted to punch Marek, so Roddy grabbed his sleeve. "Calm down," he said. "If it matters to you, then of course we'll help find it. It can't have gone far, can it?"

"Is this it?" said Geno. He was holding a limp, rather grubby sock in his hand.

Jimmy looked as if Geno had produced a rabbit out of a hat. "Where was it?" he asked, grabbing it from him and examining it carefully.

"Just here, behind the door," said Geno mildly. "It must have fallen onto the floor when you got out of bed this morning and got kicked over here by mistake."

"You know a sock can't *really* bring you luck," said Roddy carefully.

"This one can," insisted Jimmy. "And *not* having it can bring bad luck."

"How do you work that one out?" asked Marek.

"It just does, all right?" said Jimmy.

Charlton House

"Some footballers *are* very superstitious," said Geno. "My dad used to play with someone who had to check the studs on his boots in the same order before each match."

"That's silly," said Marek.

"But my dad reckoned that if you believe in these things and then don't do them one day it *can* affect your game, just because you believe it will," said Geno. "He told me never to be superstitious, because once you start you can never stop."

"Well, we'd better make sure you don't lose you sock again then, hadn't we?" said Roddy. "We don't want you freaking out like this before a match."

"You won't tell anyone else, will you?" said Jimmy. "Only I'd be sure to get teased, and then I'd lose my temper and hit someone and get into trouble and…"

"OK, OK!" said Roddy. "We get the idea.

Long Shot

Just look after your sock better." He looked at the expression on Jimmy's face and sighed.

"Why don't you keep it in your wardrobe?" suggested Geno.

Roddy nodded encouragingly. After all, Jimmy's wardrobe seemed like the most sensible place to keep a sock. "Why not put it in one of your shoes?" he asked.

"Good idea," agreed Jimmy. He burrowed into his wardrobe, and stowed his precious sock away.

"Phew," said Roddy. "Now we can all get back to normal."

But Roddy spoke too soon because the very next day, when Jimmy went to the wardrobe, his sock was missing. And his football boots had gone, too!

4. Yellow Card

Jimmy glared wildly at his three roommates. "One of you has hidden my boots to wind me up!" he shouted. "Where are they?"

"None of us wants to wind you up," said Roddy. "You go off like a rocket as it is!"

"And I'm sorry I suggested the wardrobe for your sock, OK?" said Geno. "I didn't know you were going to put it in your *football* boot. You know we're supposed to keep our boots downstairs."

"Don't worry," said Roddy. "They'll be somewhere. In fact, I bet Mr Clutterbuck has taken them. One of the cleaners probably told him."

"But they were in my wardrobe," protested

Long Shot

Jimmy. "How would anyone know the boots were there?"

"You've been tracking mud up the stairs and into our room for days," Geno pointed out. "It's like you were laying a trail for the cleaners."

"Let's go and see Mr Clutterbuck," said Roddy. "I'm sure he'll give you the sock back. After all, it's only boots that are supposed to be kept downstairs."

"No, it's all right," said Jimmy. "It's my problem. I'll go on my own."

A few minutes later, Jimmy returned looking very sheepish.

"Well?" said Marek.

"I got the sock," said Jimmy. "But Mr Clutterbuck gave me a lecture about leaving mud everywhere. He said he wouldn't give me a yellow card this time, though."

"Thank goodness!" said Roddy.

"But he will if I do it again," Jimmy added. He pulled the sock out of his pocket and put it back under his pillow. No one said anything, but Roddy sincerely hoped that the sock wouldn't go walkabout again.

For a few days, they all kept half an eye on Jimmy and his sock, but there were no more dramas. It was just as well, because there was a lot going on.

Roddy was trying hard to perform well in training so that he would be sure of a place in the first team. Stadium School played against some of the best youth sides in the country, and it would be a huge honour to get picked. The only problem was, he would be competing against everyone in the year.

It was a different story within Charlton House, because there weren't so many students to choose from.

Long Shot

Roddy and Keira soon started to create a really useful footballing partnership. They were developing an understanding on the pitch that would hopefully pay dividends in the House Cup. In a surprisingly even friendly, between the Charlton first and second years, they combined to devastating effect, scoring a goal each and setting up another two for Geno. David was extremely impressed, and told them so after the game.

"It's great to see the two of you working together and not trying to win the game on your own. You don't always have to play the Hollywood pass. Sometimes it's best to just lay it off to a team-mate. The two of you have done well to pick that up so young."

As he showered, Roddy couldn't help feeling a glow of pride. If the head of Charlton House was impressed, it was surely a good sign for his chances next term for the first team!

Yellow Card

Things weren't going quite so well in the classroom. Roddy was trying his best, but he was never going to be a high flyer as far as schoolwork went. And for no reason that he could understand, their science teacher seemed to have taken a disliking to him.

"Are you a follower of modern art, Jones?" said Mr Mustard, before he gave back their exercise books.

"Me?" said Roddy. "No, I don't think so."

"You don't think so," repeated the teacher. "Don't you know?" He didn't wait for an answer. "You were supposed to give me a diagram of the eye. A *scientific* drawing, not a poor copy of a Picasso on one of his off-days."

The exercise book landed on Roddy's desk with an accusatory flop, to the accompaniment of muted laughter from Jack's direction.

"Since when does a diagram of an eye have eyelashes?" said Mr Mustard.

Long Shot

More people started laughing and Roddy felt himself blush. He'd only drawn the eyelashes on as a joke, to amuse Geno during homework. He must have forgotten to rub them out.

"Yellow card," added Mr Mustard flatly. "And you'll get a red one if you try to make a mockery of my lessons again."

There was a shocked silence as everyone absorbed what he'd just said. Roddy felt terrible. He was the first person in their year to be carded. Now he'd have to throw himself into practice sessions even more, and hope Charlton could pull off a win in their first match.

Almost everyone sympathised with Roddy after the lesson, even those who were in different houses, and would benefit from his mistake.

"Very harsh," said Ali, who was in Banks.

Yellow Card

"I'm sorry," Roddy apologised to his fellow Charltons. But Geno, Jimmy, Marek, Keira and others rallied round him.

"It wasn't fair," said Geno loyally. "Maybe I should have owned up that it was me who encouraged you to do it."

"No way!" said Keira. "You might have got a yellow card as well!"

"It's early days," said Jimmy. "We'll make up the points again."

"I hope so," said Roddy.

The only person who scoffed at Roddy's misfortune was Jack. "Roddy Jones is the first to let his house down," he laughed. "You're going to be really popular now. Loser Jones. That's your new name!"

"Take no notice," advised Keira. "He's not worth it. Come on. It's almost time for the seniors' match. Let's go and cheer them on."

Unfortunately, Charlton seniors were

Long Shot

playing Stiles, which meant that Jack would be there supporting his team as well. Roddy chose a spot as far away from him as possible, but just before the match started, Jack made his way down the field so that he was standing opposite Roddy.

"Just ignore him," urged Geno as Jack's chant of *Loooser, Loooser* drifted across the pitch.

Roddy knew it was good advice, but it was hard not to react, especially with so many people around to hear Jack's insults.

As the teams ran on, a huge cheer went up from both groups of supporters, and Jack stopped his taunting. Charlton seniors had beaten Stiles several times before, so they were expecting another win. With his ten points to make up, Roddy really hoped they could pull it off today. David Leval was there at the head of the Charlton team, and Roddy recognised a few of the other, older students, too.

From the kickoff, Charlton were playing quick, expansive football and really making the Stiles players chase the ball. Pretty soon they were ahead, with a well-worked goal, finished off by David himself. The rest of the half went by with Charlton controlling the game, and their goalie hardly having to touch the ball at all.

Stiles began the second half much more brightly, and even managed an equaliser, but Charlton's superior class shone through and they scored another two goals before the final whistle, leaving the final score 3–1.

Charlton House went in for tea feeling well satisfied. After a few nail-biting moments, the seniors had managed a convincing win. This was an excellent start to the House Cup tournament.

Long Shot

"Great result! Shame we didn't get the bonus points for a clean sheet though. What we need now is for Moore to lose in their first game," a Charlton boy in front of Roddy said. "Moore is always the hardest house to beat."

"And if we're to have a real chance of beating them overall, we desperately need the juniors to come good. We don't want any idiots picking up yellow cards," another boy added.

Roddy bit his lip. He had been thrilled at the win, but his high spirits soon evaporated as he remembered that at the moment he was more of a hindrance to his house than a help.

5. First Match Fever

Roddy kept his head down as far as lessons went for the next few weeks. He was determined not to be given any more yellow cards. He got on fine with most of the teachers, and they could see he was doing his best, but Mr Mustard was another matter. It seemed that whatever Roddy did, he was in the wrong. Worse still, Mr Mustard liked Jack, who was really good at science. And Jack lost no time in goading Roddy about it. He even started making unkind remarks about Roddy's work during lessons, and Mr Mustard never told him off.

Several times, it was on the tip of Roddy's tongue to defend himself, but he resisted.

Long Shot

He was afraid that if he responded he'd end up with another yellow card, while Jack would get off scot free.

Several of Roddy's friends suggested that he should complain to Mr Clutterbuck, but Roddy refused.

"It wouldn't do any good," he told Geno. "Teachers stick together, don't they? No, I'll just weather it. I'm not going to give anybody an excuse to give me another yellow card."

Meanwhile, the older years had been racking up points in the House Cup. Charlton had been performing well. They were firmly in second place as things stood; a good few points ahead of Stiles and Banks, but still lagging behind Moore, who had made an excellent start to the season. The senior teams had already played two games, as had the juniors, and now it was the turn of the first years.

First Match Fever

Roddy didn't need to check his fixtures calendar to know that Charlton were up against Banks – he'd been looking forward to the match since the first day of term and especially enjoyed the past week of intensive training. He was a little apprehensive about playing in his first match for his house, but with Keira, Geno, Jimmy and Marek by his side, they were pretty confident of a win.

The only real downer for Roddy was that Sam had chosen Keira to be captain, and not him. He realised that the yellow card he'd got from Mr Mustard had not helped his chances, and he tried his best not to feel jealous. Keira deserved her position – she was a good motivator, her enthusiasm was infectious, and she worked really hard. But not being captain was a new experience for Roddy, and he knew he'd find it hard to be told what to do by his midfield partner.

Long Shot

Sam had chosen the attacking formation that they'd worked on in training the day before, allowing both Roddy and Keira to make their incisive runs. Jimmy was playing in central defence as part of a back three, and the twins Eboni and Ashanti were in their natural positions on either wing.

Because of the way the houses were divided, Charlton didn't have a strong defensive team, but David and Sam had explained that the Charlton ethos was to play quick, attacking football, aiming to put as many goals past the opposition as possible. And with Marcel Temperley in goal, it was unlikely their team would let many in, either.

Roddy felt the familiar buzz as he jogged onto the pitch. He was wearing the ankle support his friend Bryn had given him, although fortunately his ankle was fine now and he was really just wearing it for insurance.

First Match Fever

The students had turned out in good numbers to support their teams, but in Roddy's mind there were several thousand fans packed into the grounds to cheer them on. As he waited, his mind started to drift.

It's almost time for kickoff, and the surprise is that Jones has lost his captain's armband to newcomer Sanders. The captains shake hands in the centre circle and toss the coin with the ref. Banks win, and will kick off the first half. Their captain retreats to his position in goal, the ref blows his whistle, and the game begins! Charlton are looking like going all-out for victory in their first game, and have set up in a 3–5–2 formation with plenty of pace up front. Banks will be doing well to contain their opponents today, but they could be dangerous on the counterattack.

From the outset, Charlton are making good use of the ball, and forcing Banks to

Long Shot

chase them. Jones and Sanders are moving it about brilliantly, and surely it can only be a matter of time before the floodgates open.

Jones on the ball. He feeds it out right to Ashanti Nagel on the wing. Nagel knocks the ball past the full-back and uses her pace to pull away from him before firing a cross into the penalty area. It's a little long, and the ball sails over everyone, but her twin is waiting on the opposite flank and pulls it back to the edge of the area. Sanders has seen the opportunity, and arrives just in time to send a shot screaming into the roof of the net from 20 yards. A fantastic finish by the Charlton captain.

The team clustered together to congratulate Keira on her goal, but she waved them away. "The game's not over yet, we've got to keep focused," she said. "Come on, let's score another one!"

First Match Fever

Banks kick off, and now we'll see what they're really made of. They're a goal down, but can they pull it back? Their captain is shouting instructions from the goalmouth. Conceding may just have spurred them into action. Jones is battling away in midfield, showing real tenacity for a player without huge physical presence, but he can't contend with some of the larger players, and is muscled off the ball.

Banks are breaking towards the Charlton goal now, and the three Charlton defenders look vulnerable. Piper comes charging out of defence, and launches himself at the ball. It looked like he might have taken out the player, too, but the ref judges it to be a clean tackle and Piper gets away with it. He was lucky there – a different referee might have given a foul. As it is, the ball is collected by Mbeki and Banks are on the back foot again.

Long Shot

"Great tackle, Jimmy, but be careful!" warned Keira when she was within shouting distance. "You don't want to get sent off – you'll miss the game against Stiles!"

Charlton seem happy just to keep possession for now, passing the ball around as if they were on the training ground. At the same time, Banks seem to be employing a plan of tight defence, hoping to nick a goal on the counterattack. It's effective football, but not the most exciting stuff.

Sam was shouting instructions from the touchline, and was pleased with how things were shaping up.

"Keep it together, and don't do anything stupid. It's only a few minutes to half-time, just hold onto the ball."

With neither side looking like altering the score, Charlton will definitely be the happier side. They're a goal up, and looking good for

First Match Fever

the win. The whistle goes, and the teams walk off for a few minutes rest.

The Charlton players stood in a ragged circle by the side of the pitch to catch their breath, which steamed in the chilly air.

Eboni was rubbing her shin, which had been kicked in an untidy tackle, but apart from that the team were in great shape. They swigged energy drinks, while Sam gave them her opinion of their first-half performance.

"Well done. You're ahead in your first house match, and the way you're playing, you should win. Just make sure you don't let them get back into the game. Another goal or two would be brilliant, but don't forget about defending.

"Keira, great goal and it's good to see your leadership on the pitch, keep it up. Now get out there and let them have it!"

The second half begins, and Charlton seem

Long Shot

really fired up. They are pressing for another goal right from the start, and that's what we like to see. Jones and Sanders are continuing to wreak havoc in the Banks half. Charlton have a free kick in a dangerous area, and Sanders is letting Jones take it. He waits a moment to assess the situation, sees Dvorski's run, and plants the ball squarely on his forehead. The keeper manages to parry the header, but Perotti is waiting to tap in the rebound! 2–0 to Charlton!

The rest of the match played out without either side creating many chances, and Charlton was happy to sit on their two-goal lead. Eboni and Ashanti operated as wing-backs so Charlton had five in defence, and Marcel Temperley in goal hardly touched the ball. The final whistle blew, and Sam went up to congratulate the team.

"You did it! That's a fantastic start. A 2–0

First Match Fever

win plus the bonus points for a clean sheet is a great result. It might even have given us a lead in the competition overall when we look at the points. But this will be one of the easiest games you play – don't think you'll beat everyone so easily. We've got Moore next, and they're going to be our main rivals for the cup, so it's vital to keep up the hard work in training. Well done, though, and enjoy your first victory!"

Keira went round the players, too, congratulating everyone. When she got to Roddy, she looked him straight in the eye. "Couldn't have done it without you," she said. "We make a great team, don't we?"

Roddy nodded. He'd certainly hated not being captain, but it was easy to support Keira. "You led us really well," he said, and meant it.

"Thanks!" said Keira, looking both pleased and relieved.

Long Shot

Roddy headed back to the boarding house with his roommates. They were going to be buzzing all night, and with good reason. Charlton had won their first house match!

6. Hallowe'en Horrors

Spirits rose as half term approached. Roddy was looking forward to seeing his family again – even his older sister Liz. And it would be great to catch up with Bryn, his best friend at home. Although they had texted each other quite a lot at the beginning of term, they had been keeping in touch less and less. They were both busy with their own lives.

It would be Hallowe'en over half term, but a few spooky bits and pieces had appeared to decorate the common room. There were masks, blow-up ghouls and even a few rubber bats. Jimmy did his best to ignore them, but Roddy could see that they irritated him.

At evening registration, the night before

Long Shot

the holiday, Jack flapped a rubber bat in Jimmy's face, completely taking him by surprise.

"Get it off me!" he told Jack, his voice shaking. "You're such an idiot!"

Several people laughed at that and Jack got angry, too. For a moment, it looked as if things might turn nasty, but Mr Clutterbuck arrived and the moment passed.

Afterwards, as Roddy and his roommates left the common room, Jack lunged towards Jimmy, brandishing the bat again. "Scared of ghosts and ghoulies, are you?" he jeered.

"Don't react," said Roddy. Grabbing onto his friend's sleeve was becoming something of a habit. "He'd love it if you got into trouble." Roddy glared at Jack as they passed. His friend hadn't got into trouble for fighting yet, but with Jack goading him, he worried that it was only a matter of time.

Hallowe'en Horrors

Back in their room, the boys each packed a small bag, so they would be ready for their parents to collect them in the morning.

"What are you doing over half term, Marek?" asked Roddy. "Are you going back to Poland?"

Marek shook his head. "My cousin will collect me," he said. "He lives in London. I will stay with him and his family."

"Sounds good," said Roddy.

After lights out, Roddy thought about what he would do in the week ahead. But it seemed not everyone was thinking of home.

"When we come back, we must win our match against Moore," said Jimmy's voice in the dark. "So we can improve our lead in the House Cup."

"Yes," agreed Roddy. They'd all worked hard this half term and things were going really well. It was great to be going home,

Long Shot

but he knew already that he would miss the excitement of Stadium School.

Roddy woke up with a start. It was pitch black in the room, and very quiet. For a moment he lay there, wondering what had woken him. Then a slight sound near Jimmy's bed made him turn his head.

His heart started thumping, and Roddy caught his breath. A terrible, glowing, greenish face was hovering there in the darkness. It was such a shock, he couldn't think straight. Then, just when he'd worked out what it must be, Jimmy woke up.

The frightened boy let out a blood-curdling scream as the face bent towards him. Roddy hurried to switch on his bedside lamp, but Jimmy's ordeal wasn't over yet. The ghost, in a white sheet and Hallowe'en mask, had got hold of Jimmy's pillow. Roddy immediately thought of the precious sock. And then he saw it, dangling from inside the pillowcase.

So did Jimmy.

"My SOCK!" Jimmy's anguished cry filled the room and the "ghost" paused in obvious surprise.

Both Marek and Geno were awake now, and Geno leaped out of bed to tear the ghost's sheet away. They grappled together for a couple of minutes, but Geno wasn't going to let go, and eventually he yanked off the disguise. The disrobed ghost swiped at Geno's head with Jimmy's pillow, missed and then stood in front of them breathing heavily.

"Jack!" they shouted.

"Stop messing around," said Roddy angrily. "Give Jimmy his sock back."

"What sock?" Jack bent to pick up his mask and the sock dropped onto the floor.

Jimmy got out of bed and rushed at Jack,

Long Shot

who was sent crashing. They wrestled for a few moments and feathers from the pillow flew up into the air.

"Stop it!" yelled Roddy. He and Marek hurried to pull them apart, but a jab from Jimmy's elbow caught Roddy in the face by mistake. "Ow! Just stop it, will you?"

Marek hauled Jack to his feet and stood him against the wall. "Where is Jimmy's sock?" he asked in a menacing voice.

"I don't know," whined Jack. "I just came in to play a Hallowe'en trick. There's no need to get so aggressive."

"I've got it," said Jimmy. He stood up. There were feathers in his hair and he looked pale with fright, but the sock was safely clutched to his chest.

"Ah! Jimmy's in love with a sock!" laughed Jack.

"Just get out," ordered Marek, fiercely.

Hallowe'en Horrors

"Jimmy's in love with a sock! Jimmy's in love with a sock!" Jack gathered his sheet and headed for the door. He slammed it behind him and Roddy let out a huge sigh of relief.

"Well, that's—" But he stopped mid-sentence as he heard Mr Clutterbuck's voice in the corridor. "Get into bed!" he hissed.

They hurried to put the sheets and pillows back in order. Roddy switched out the light and they all lay silently, ears straining to hear what the housemaster was saying. They couldn't hear the words, but they did hear Jack's voice a couple of times, and then Mr Clutterbuck's again, louder and sounding very angry.

"Half term or no half term, you're not allowed to go wandering into other people's bedrooms in the middle of the night," he said.

Roddy allowed himself a slight smile. It was never a good idea to argue with a teacher.

Long Shot

There was silence again, and Roddy started to think it was all over, but then the door opened, and he could see the shape of Mr Clutterbuck, outlined against the light in the corridor.

"Any more people looking for a yellow card?" he said. The four boys stayed quiet and after a moment he closed the door again. They waited until his footsteps faded away and then Jimmy spoke.

"Jack's got a yellow card. Good! Serves him right."

"Thank goodness Clutterbuck didn't catch you fighting, Jimmy," said Roddy quietly. "Otherwise you'd have got one, too."

Around mid morning, Roddy's father arrived to take him home. "Bye!" he called to Geno and Keira, who were still waiting for their parents. "Have a good one. See you soon!" He slung his

Hallowe'en Horrors

bag into the back of the car and got in.

"Well? How's it been?" His dad was looking at him anxiously.

Roddy sank back in his seat. "Brilliant!" he said with a broad grin.

The journey home passed quickly, with Roddy telling his dad about everything that had happened since he'd got to Stadium School.

As soon as the car stopped outside their house, Roddy leaped out. His sister opened the door and his mum gave him a big hug.

"It's wonderful to have you back home," she said. "And I'm sure you've grown."

"Mum!" Roddy complained, wriggling out of her arms. But she was right. It *was* good to be back.

It wasn't long before he slipped back into his old way of life. He went round his room, reacquainting himself with all his belongings.

Long Shot

He earmarked a couple of computer games to take back to school with him, and three books he'd been given and not read.

The next morning he texted Bryn. *I'm back! R U free? Want 2 go 2 the park?*

Yeah. C U at yrs in 10.

Very soon, Bryn was at the front door, beaming all over his face. "How's it going? Have you been spotted yet?" he said.

"No, don't be daft. We only played our first match last week. We won it, though, 2–0! And our house is winning overall in the cup at the moment, but not by much. Are you in the school team?"

"Yeah, it's brilliant. Shame we haven't got you playing for us, but I'm glad you're doing well at Stadium School. Hey, there's a Hallowe'en party at one of my mates' houses tomorrow. Want to come?"

"You bet! Hang on a minute, though.

Hallowe'en Horrors

I've got something for you."

Bryn waited while Roddy tore up to his room and back down the stairs again. "What is it?"

"Two linesman's flags," said Roddy, holding them out. "They got new ones this term and these were going to be chucked out. Mr Jenkins said I could have them. They say Stadium School on them," he added anxiously, not sure now if it had been a good idea to bring them for his friend or not.

But Bryn was delighted. "That's so cool!" he said. "I'll put them up in my room, on either side of my England poster. Thanks, mate."

Bryn was really interested to hear about the house competition. "We've got something like that, too," he said, "except ours is for sports and art and music and drama, and all sorts of stuff. What are your teachers like?"

"They're OK," replied Roddy with a shrug.

Long Shot

"Apart from this one called Mr Mustard. He hates me, and gave me a yellow card for nothing."

"I reckon every school has one like him," Bryn told him. "Our history teacher is the same. I've made some good friends, though. How about you?"

Roddy told him about Jimmy, Marek and Geno.

"They sound cool," Bryn said. "Have you met Geno's famous dad yet?"

"No," replied Roddy. "Not yet. But maybe I will at the end of term."

"Shall we go to the park, then?" suggested Bryn, suddenly changing the subject.

Roddy grinned. "Yeah! Let's do that."

At the park, Roddy showed Bryn some of the tactics he'd learned. Soon there was a whole group of people there. Roddy knew most of them from his old school, and in no

Hallowe'en Horrors

time they were playing a game. It was almost like old times.

What with parties, football and family time, the week sped by. Soon there were only two days to go, and then only one. Roddy's mum cooked a special meal for his last night, and they all had a family evening together.

Just before he went up to bed, Roddy's mum took him to one side. "I'm so pleased everything is going well for you," she said. "But don't forget, if you need us, we're only at the other end of the phone."

"Mum!" Roddy gave her a look. "I'm fine! In fact, I'm having the best time *ever*. Thanks so much for finding the money to send me to Stadium School. I know it wasn't easy."

Roddy's mum gave him a hug and they said goodnight. But Roddy was so excited, he couldn't sleep. His week at home had been

Long Shot

brilliant, but he couldn't wait to get back to Stadium School and find out what the next half term had in store...

7. Back At School

It was straight back to work. Roddy had resolved to get on Mr Mustard's right side, and things were slowly improving. At last, the teacher gave him a "much better" comment on his homework, and Roddy hoped that Mr Mustard had begun to see him in a better light.

Sam's senior girls' team were playing Stiles just a few days after they got back, and as they were currently in third place, Sam was really chasing a win to lift them up the table. Roddy and several other members of the Charlton junior squad headed over to the pitch to support their coach, but it was the Stiles fans who were cheering loudest at the end of the game.

Long Shot

Despite Sam's efforts, Charlton lost 2–0, leaving them stuck in third place with only Moore behind them. In the context of the overall House Cup, not much was changed, with Moore losing to Banks the same day, but Sam's disappointment at her own team's fortunes was noticeable at training the next day. Roddy knew that their next result had to be a good one, if only to cheer up Sam.

It was still over six weeks until Christmas, but Marek already knew what he wanted from his parents. "I'm going to ask for the new Poland strip," he said. "What are you going to ask for?"

"I'm not sure," said Roddy. With money tight at home he didn't want to be too greedy.

Their next match was against Moore, who had recently seen their lead in the House Cup

Back At School

evaporate, with losses from their senior teams. Now it was Charlton who were ahead in the contest, so a victory against them would help to open up the gap.

"I watched some of the Moore first-year game against Stiles," said Sam. "Moore slaughtered them. Don't worry, though – I think you can beat them, but you'll need to work hard to pull it off."

"You heard," said Keira to her team. "We've got to go all out for this one. Good luck, everyone. Keep your heads up and we can do it. Charlton for ever!"

"Charlton for ever!"

As Roddy ran onto the pitch, he felt totally fired up, and almost straight away the commentary inside his head took over.

Moore kick off, and they're already forcing Charlton back towards their own goal. This could be a tough day for the Charlton defence,

Long Shot

but Piper gets in there with a magnificent tackle to dispossess the Moore forward and start Charlton on the counterattack. Jones has the ball at his feet now, and sets off on a run. He moves the ball to Sanders, and gets it back seconds later. Perotti is calling for it ahead of him, and Jones sends it straight to his feet. Perotti unleashes the shot, but the keeper makes a comfortable save.

Roddy's team were under a lot of pressure, and relying on quick breaks to get any chances to score. Eboni and Ashanti were spending almost all their time helping out in defence, and Jimmy was working harder than anyone, marshalling the rearguard effort. The team struggled their way to half time, and sat exhausted, while Sam tried to raise their spirits.

"You're playing well," she said. "Moore are a strong team. To be honest, a draw would be a good result today, but if you can nick a goal that would be brilliant. Jimmy, you're doing great work organising the defence, but if you can, try passing it out rather than sending long balls down to Marek and Geno all the time. I know it's hard when you're under pressure, but if you can get it to Eboni or Ashanti we might catch them on the break. Good luck!"

The teams are coming back out onto the pitch for the second half, and neither side has made any substitutions. The whistle blows, and Charlton are under heavy pressure again, with most of the action taking place in and around their penalty area. Piper gets in another good challenge, and passes out to his winger on the left. Nagel gets skilfully past her man, and suddenly she has space to run. Nagel sprints down the left wing and sends in a perfect cross to Dvorski. Dvorski powers a header straight towards the top corner, but the Moore keeper pulls off yet another fantastic save to deny the

Long Shot

lanky striker, and tips it over the bar. Corner to Charlton!

Charlton are throwing a lot of players forward. Jones is loitering outside the box, as Sanders goes to take the corner. She plays it short to Nagel, who sends in the cross. It's too deep for Dvorski, and too high for Perotti. The full-back gets to it before anyone else and punts it away down the pitch.

Jones is sprinting back to cover, but the Moore forwards have the ball and Piper is all alone. He's backing off, caught in two minds whether to close down the player with the ball or mark the other striker. Things look grim for Charlton, but suddenly Piper launches himself at the ball and wins it. Absolute brilliance from Piper there. He's saved an almost certain goal!

Roddy had time to give Jimmy a quick thumbs up before collecting the ball. He was panting hard, but dared not let up. As soon as he started running, he was in danger of being closed down, so he looked for space to pass the ball on.

Jones collects the loose ball, and heads back up the other end of the pitch. His work rate today has been outstanding. This match is really starting to open out in the final minutes. Nagel receives the ball wide on the right, but is tackled. The ball bobbles loose, then goes out of play for a Charlton corner. Even Piper is coming up for this one! Sanders is asking Jones to take the corner. He crosses the ball beautifully, and it falls to Piper, who lashes it home! 1–0 to Charlton! Piper is the hero of this game, no doubt about it! His team-mates crowd around him, and the Moore players look gutted. They've dominated this game, but Piper kept Charlton in it, then scored the winner off Jones's inspired cross!

The ref restarted the game but, with only a

Long Shot

minute left, both sets of players knew it was all over. After the final whistle, Roddy came off the field, as elated at the rest of the Charlton team.

"Thanks for giving me the corner," he said to Keira. "I enjoyed taking it."

"You're better at them than me," she said. "Especially from that side. And we wouldn't have got the goal without your cross."

Sam was there to congratulate them as they left the field.

"That was brilliant, Jimmy! Some of the best defending I've seen for ages, and your goal was just the icing on the cake. Great cross from you, too, Roddy. You've all done fantastically well to win today. Don't forget though, the house competition's fifteen games long, not two. There's a long way to go yet. But well done for today. Now, go and get showered!"

8. Jimmy's Ordeal

Roddy threw his dirty kit into the washing basket. It was starting to become a habit to meet up in the team talk room after a match, so as soon as he was dressed, Roddy went through to see who was there. A lot of people had gone to get their tea first, but Keira was slumped at the table looking happy but exhausted. Roddy grabbed a cup of water and went over to join her.

"That's the hardest we've had to work so far," he said. "But it was a great result. Don't you think, Jimmy?" he added to his friend, who had just appeared.

Jimmy didn't reply. Instead he sat down with his head bowed.

Long Shot

"You were great today," Roddy went on. "You won the match for us. I still can't believe we did it... Jimmy?"

There was no reply. Instead, Jimmy just sat there. Roddy felt a horrible sense of misgiving. He'd been fine during the match, and afterwards. What could possibly be wrong now?

Roddy touched Jimmy's arm. "Are you OK?"

Jimmy didn't look at Roddy, he just handed him a crumpled piece of paper.

IF YOU WANT YOUR LUCK BACK, YOU'LL FIND IT AT THE STADIUM SEATS. MAKE SURE YOU COME DOWN THE TUNNEL ALONE AT MIDNIGHT TONIGHT OR IT WILL BE DESTROYED. TELL NO ONE.

Roddy groaned. "Oh no!"

Jimmy's Ordeal

"What is it?" asked Keira.

Jimmy tried to snatch the paper back, but Roddy pushed his hand away.

"Anything that affects you, affects the team," he said. He passed the note to Keira, who read it quickly and then bit her lip.

"I realised you were a bit superstitious from when we took Marek to the tree tunnel," she mused. "But this is blackmail. What's going on?"

Jimmy explained about the lucky sock. He sounded both angry and embarrassed. "I didn't want anyone else to know," he said. "I feel such an idiot."

"But Roddy's right," said Keira. "We're team-mates aren't we? We have to stick together and decide what to do for the best. Who do you think wrote the note?"

"It's Jack," said Roddy flatly. "It has to be. Stiles didn't have a match today. He must have

Long Shot

sneaked in and left it here while we were playing. Has the sock gone?" he asked, knowing what the answer would be.

Jimmy nodded. "I went to check," he said mournfully.

"He's just trying to wind you up, Jimmy," said Keira. "Don't let it get to you. Why don't you take the note to Mr Clutterbuck? He'll sort it out."

"I can't, can I?" said Jimmy miserably. "If I do, the sock will be destroyed." He shivered. "I shouldn't have told any of you."

"For goodness' sake. Get a grip," said Roddy. "Jack's not all-powerful. He can't tell what's going on everywhere." But Jimmy glanced fearfully at the door and Roddy couldn't help doing so, too.

He shook his head angrily. "You've got me at it now," he complained.

As soon as the rest of the team arrived,

they could see that something was wrong, but it took a while before Roddy could persuade Jimmy he needed to take them into his confidence, too. "*I'll* tell them, and then you won't need to," he coaxed. "The note is just for you. It doesn't say *nobody* must tell *anyone*."

"All right," said Jimmy, anxiously biting his lip.

They all sat as far away from the door as they could to reassure Jimmy that nobody could overhear, and held a council of war. But no matter what they said, Jimmy was determined to carry out the instructions in the note.

"But you were too scared to walk down the tunnel with us in the *daytime*," Geno reminded him bluntly. "How are you going to manage it in the dark, at midnight, on your own?"

Long Shot

Jimmy looked at Geno with frightened eyes. "It's a *test*." he said. "It's about how much it matters to me, isn't it? I've *got* to do it."

"What about when you're caught and given a yellow card?" said Marek. "No, it'll probably be a *red* card for being out so late at night. That must be Jack's plan, to get you banned for our game against Stiles. We need you in the side, Jimmy. Are you going to throw our chances away ... for a sock!"

"It's not just *any* old sock," said Jimmy fiercely.

Eventually, after loads of talking they managed to get him to agree to do nothing that night.

"If you go there first thing in the morning, I'm sure you'll find it," said Keira. "Jack isn't going to risk getting a red card himself. He'll just put the sock on the seats and be sniggering to himself about you agonising over it. He knows you don't like spooky things, so he's sure you'll be freaked out. He's probably hoping you'll go to pieces and be hopeless when we play them next, but you won't be, because you'll have your sock back safe and sound."

"At last! You've seen sense," said Roddy. "Thank goodness for that!"

"And from now on we'll all keep a close eye on Jack," said Keira. "If he tries on anything with any of you, don't keep it to yourselves, whatever you do. We're much stronger as a team."

Those who hadn't eaten tea yet went inside in a much lighter frame of mind, although Roddy noticed that, unusually for him, Jimmy ate very little.

Jack was in the dining room, and Roddy would have loved to have gone over and

Long Shot

punched him on the nose, but Jimmy had made them all promise to say and do nothing. Besides, Roddy had to keep reminding himself that there wasn't any proof that Jack was behind it.

Everyone was tired after the match. Quite soon, they all headed back to their rooms to relax. Roddy and his roommates were all in bed before lights out, and nobody felt like talking.

"All right, Jimmy?" asked Roddy before they went to sleep.

"All right," a small voice replied.

Roddy wondered if he ought to stay awake for a bit, in case Jimmy wanted to talk. But he was tired, and soon his eyes closed. It was much later when he felt a hand shaking his shoulder. He had been dreaming he was the only player against a whole team made up of Jacks. "What is it?" he asked, trying to rid himself of the image.

"It's Jimmy," said Geno. "He's gone!"

Roddy woke from one nightmare and was plunged into another. "Maybe he's just gone to the bathroom," he suggested, struggling to sit up.

"Marek's just been to check," said Geno. "He's not there. And his trainers have gone."

Roddy groaned.

"Shall we tell Mr Clutterbuck?" said Geno.

"If we do, Jimmy will get a red card," said Marek.

"We can't guarantee Mr C will find out who wrote the note and punish them," added Roddy.

"You're right," agreed Geno. "And that's the last thing we want."

Roddy thought quickly. He pulled on his tracksuit over his pyjamas and grabbed his trainers. "I'm going to go and find him,"

Long Shot

he said. "He'll be a gibbering idiot out there on his own. But if I'm quick, maybe I can get the sock and bring Jimmy back indoors without anyone seeing us."

"But if you get caught, that will be two red cards," said Marek. "And there's no way we'll win our next match. We won't beat Stiles with two players down."

"Jimmy will spend all night trying to pluck up the courage to fetch his stupid sock," argued Roddy. "He'll *definitely* get caught. If I nip out and get it for him, we'll have a good chance of getting away with it. Look, I can climb out of this window, no bother. It faces away from Mr Clutterbuck's part of the house."

"Isn't it too high?" said Geno. "We're on the first floor."

"But the ground rises, too," said Roddy. "I'll be fine."

Jimmy's Ordeal

Geno started pulling on his tracksuit.

"What are you doing?" said Roddy.

"Coming with you."

"That's stupid."

"No, it's not," said Geno. "Jimmy will throw a wobbly if you insist on going down the tunnel, because the note said he had to go alone. But if you go round the back of the main building, straight to the pitch end of the tunnel, you can collect the sock, sprint up the tunnel to us, and the job will be done before Jimmy realises. Just in case anything holds you up, I'll go to the changing-room end, where Jimmy will be, and look after him until you meet us with the sock."

"That's genius!" said Roddy. "Let's do it."

"Then I'm coming, too," insisted Marek. "Because if I stay, and Mr Clutterbuck comes and asks where you are, I won't know what to say."

Long Shot

There didn't seem any point in arguing. They all turned their pillows round in their beds so it looked as if they were still there, then Roddy opened the window and they climbed out, one by one.

The grass was very wet, and they were slightly worried about their shoes leaving tell-tale tracks in the dew, but it couldn't be helped. Roddy and Marek set off towards the Stadium pitch, while Geno headed for the changing rooms.

As they approached the main building, Roddy heard a car door slam. "Wait!" he hissed to Marek. They crouched down behind some bushes and paused while someone started up a car.

"One of the teachers must have guests," whispered Marek.

"Oh no!" groaned Roddy. "It's Mr Mustard. If he sees us, I'm done for!"

Jimmy's Ordeal

The boys watched as the teacher got into his car and started it up. For a moment, the headlights lit up the bushes they were hiding behind. They held their breath, but the car drove on, down the drive and towards the main road.

Roddy and Marek got up cautiously. "Come on. Let's get this over with," said Roddy. "What are you doing?" he added.

Marek was retrieving a football from where it had got wedged in the bushes.

"It's a shame to leave this here," Marek explained. "It's a good ball. I'll take it to lost property in the morning."

Roddy sighed, but waited for Marek to join him, then together they approached the Stadium pitch.

"What's that?" whispered Roddy. He pointed towards something moving amongst the preserved seats.

Long Shot

"It must be Jimmy!" said Marek. "He's done it – he's gone down the tunnel! Well done him!"

He was just about to speed towards the figure, when Roddy stopped him. "Wait a moment," he whispered. "That doesn't look like Jimmy! But then who *is* it? And what are they doing?"

The figure *did* look rather strange. It was difficult to see in the moonlight, but it seemed to constantly change shape as it flitted between the seats. Its long clothes billowed first one way and then another in the breeze.

Marek crouched down and clutched Roddy's arm. "I have never seen a ghost before," he said quietly. "But is that one?"

Roddy didn't know what to say. Maybe the ghost stories about the school were true after all. Then he checked himself. He was being stupid! There were no such things as ghosts.

Jimmy's Ordeal

It was Jack. It had to be! It would be just like him to try to freak Jimmy out. The greenish light that illuminated the swaying figure must be Jack's torch with a filter on it.

"We need garlic," muttered Marek. "Garlic is good against ghosts."

"No, we don't," said Roddy. "It's not a ghost. I don't believe in them anyway. I bet it's Jack."

"Really?" asked Marek. He peered at the ghostly figure again. "Maybe you're right. What an idiot! He's risking a red card just to get Jimmy in trouble."

"But if Jimmy manages to get himself down the tunnel and thinks Jack is a ghost, he'll have a heart attack! Let's get a bit closer. We've got to try and stop him."

The boys made their way along the side of the pitch as quietly as possible, keeping low and stopping frequently. Luckily, their

Long Shot

tracksuits were dark and eventually they were close to the beginning of the seating.

"Can you see the sock?" whispered Marek.

"There!" Roddy whispered hoarsely. "In Jack's hand."

"What's he doing?"

"It's a fire! He's started a fire!"

To his horror, Roddy could see Jack dangling Jimmy's sock over the flames. He had to do something! With no time to think, he grabbed the football from Marek's hands, and stood up. He gave it an enormous kick, aiming to hit the sock away from the fire. But as his foot connected with the ball, something came hurtling down the tunnel with a wild, banshee wail.

Roddy, Marek and Jack whipped round to see what it was, and the ball hit Jack squarely on the back of his head. Jack dropped the sock, gave a tremendous howl, and fell over.

Jimmy's Ordeal

"We'll get the sock!" yelled Geno, who had appeared with the screaming banshee, which was actually a frantic Jimmy.

Marek leaped to his feet and ran to grab Jack, but Jack struggled to his feet and legged it up the tunnel.

"I think Jack's had more of a fright than we have tonight," said Roddy. "He thought he was going to be the only person here, apart from Jimmy."

"That shot must have *terrified* him when it hit the back of his head," Marek snorted with laughter.

"What an idiot to start a fire, though," said Roddy. "He could have burnt down the rest of the seats."

"And even the Stadium pitch!" said Jimmy sounding shocked.

"At any rate, he's made a good job of burning your sock," said Geno.

Long Shot

They all looked at the still-smouldering sock, dangling from Jimmy's hand. It was terribly charred, smelt awful, and was falling to pieces.

"Never mind," said Jimmy uncertainly. "It's probably all right."

"Listen," said Roddy slowly. "I've been thinking. You don't need that sock, and I can prove it."

"What do you mean?" said Jimmy.

"Well, remember that blinder of a match you played yesterday? At some point during the match, Jack nicked your sock. And yet you played some of your best football at the end of the game. How about that winning goal? You certainly didn't need the lucky sock then."

"No... I suppose not," Jimmy said reluctantly.

"And tonight," Roddy went on, "you came over here all by yourself, although you're terrified of ghosts. That was really brave, and you didn't have the sock to help you. You don't need that sock, really, you don't."

Jimmy looked at the smelly, charred sock and then back at Roddy. "But we're going to need a lot of luck to get back to our room," he said in a sad voice. "And if we're all caught, Charlton will probably lose the next match and maybe even the House Cup."

"The luck has run out of that sock," said Roddy firmly. He patted Jimmy on his back. "Come on. We have to make our own luck. And if we do get caught, well, we'll make sure that Jack's luck runs out, too. His trainers are going to be just as wet as ours from the grass, and with any luck he'll smell of smoke."

"He might get expelled," said Geno soberly, picking up the spooky ghost costume that Jack had left lying on the ground. "What shall we do with the stuff he left behind? There's this

Long Shot

torch with the green filter, which made him look so weird. He was really serious about scaring Jimmy, wasn't he?"

"He didn't enjoy being challenged," said Roddy. "But I don't think he'll try anything like this again."

"Let's dump everything in the bins," suggested Marek.

Jimmy took a deep breath and gave his friends a wavering smile. "I'll put the sock in with them," he said bravely. "I'm sorry I've been such a pain about it."

"It's been worth it for all that fantastic defending you do," said Roddy seriously. "Now, let's go. Follow me."

9. Red Card

"I want to go back up the tunnel."

Roddy looked at Jimmy. "Are you sure?" he asked. "It's not the quickest way, and haven't you been scared enough for one night?"

"Well, I managed to run down it," said Jimmy, "even though I was terrified. I just think it would help."

"Come on, then," said Marek. "Don't let's waste time."

Even Roddy had to admit that the tunnel was spooky at night. He couldn't help being unsettled by the leaves rustling above them, and the ever-changing shadows cast by the half moon scudding through the clouds. It seemed to take ages to get to the other end,

Long Shot

but Roddy was determined not to hurry. There was just a chance that Jack might still be lurking somewhere, and Roddy didn't want them to run into trouble.

"Do you think there is a real ghost around here?" said Geno quietly.

Roddy sighed. "Before tonight, I'd have said definitely not. And I know it was only Jack messing about back there. But there's something about this place... Something a bit creepy." He shivered. "I'm glad we're almost out of the tunnel."

Everything was still and silent as they emerged at the back of the changing rooms. Roddy noticed a bin nearby, and Marek took the lid off as quietly as he could. They stuffed Jack's ghost outfit and the torch deep inside. Then Jimmy held out his sock. He hesitated for a moment, and then let it fall in, too. Marek replaced the lid with a soft clang.

Red Card

"Well done, Jimmy," whispered Roddy.

They made it past the front of the main building, and back to their boarding house without any trouble. The whole school was sleeping, and all the windows were dark. There was no sign of Jack. He must have got back safely already. But their window seemed a long way from the ground, now they were trying to climb indoors.

"I thought the ground was higher than this," said Geno in a panicky voice, staring up at the window. "I'll never get in."

For a few moments they stood there, wondering what to do. "I'll give you each a leg up," suggested Roddy, "and then you can haul me in." But, privately, he wondered if he'd be able to manage, with no one to help him.

"I am tallest," whispered Marek. "I will be last. I can easily reach the window by myself."

Long Shot

"OK," agreed Roddy.

Jimmy and Geno were already inside, and Roddy was just scrambling up with Marek's help, when Jimmy appeared at the window and hauled him quickly through. "Someone's coming!" he hissed. "Get into bed!"

There was no time to warn Marek. And Roddy didn't wait to take off his tracksuit or trainers. He threw himself under his duvet and lay still, trying to control his breathing. Jimmy had been right. There *was* activity in the corridor outside. It sounded as if Mr Clutterbuck was going into each room in turn. But it was very late for their housemaster to be up and about.

Two doors in the corridor had already been opened and closed. It must be their turn next. Sure enough, the heavy footsteps came towards their door and it opened. Mr Clutterbuck stood there in his dressing gown.

Red Card

Roddy imagined he wouldn't be in the best of moods. To his horror, the housemaster came into the room and peered closely at Geno's supposedly sleeping form. He seemed to be satisfied but, as he straightened up, he caught sight of the half-open curtains blowing in the breeze.

Mr Clutterbuck walked over to the window. Roddy was sure Marek would be discovered. He held his breath and waited, but the housemaster simply closed the window and turned back to the door. He hesitated for a moment and then left the room, shutting it quietly behind him.

They waited for the footsteps to fade away down the corridor, then Roddy scrambled out of bed and opened the window again. Marek was standing outside, with his hands on his hips.

"Why did you close the window?" he said,

glaring at Roddy accusingly. "This is a bad time for jokes."

"Ssh!" said Roddy. "It wasn't our fault. Mr C's been here. It was him who shut the window."

"He checked all the rooms in our corridor," said Geno, throwing off his tracksuit and trainers. "It's a miracle he didn't see you."

"That was him?" said Marek in horror. "I thought it was one of you, messing about."

"Believe me," said Jimmy with feeling. "There's been enough messing about tonight to last me a lifetime!"

"I don't know how you managed to stay so still when he was peering at you," Roddy said to Geno.

"I just kept thinking of red cards," said Geno with a shudder.

"Let's get to sleep," said Jimmy. "We have to be up again in a few hours."

Red Card

Marek groaned. "I'm never going to stay awake in lessons tomorrow."

In a few moments, they were all in bed. Roddy's feet were frozen, and the ends of his pyjamas were soaking wet. But nothing could keep him awake now, and soon they were all fast asleep.

Nobody felt exactly full of beans in the morning. They crawled out of bed and stumbled into the bathroom. Roddy felt a bit better after a shower, but nothing like his usual enthusiastic self. The others were just as tired, but they *were* all anxious to see if anything would be said at registration.

Sure enough, after Mr Clutterbuck had taken the register, he didn't dismiss the students. "I just want to remind you that outside is out of bounds after bedtime," he said, looking very serious. Anyone breaking this rule will be severely punished, with a red card at the very least."

Roddy tried to get a look at Jack, but he had turned away and Roddy couldn't see his face. Unsurprisingly, most of the students in the room looked confused. They had no idea what had gone on the night before.

"Right. That will be all," said Mr Clutterbuck.

As soon as the housemaster had gone, the room erupted into loud chatter. "What was all that about?" someone asked Roddy.

Roddy shrugged. "I dunno," he lied.

It soon emerged that Jack had been caught outside after bedtime, and had got a red card for it. According to Ali, his roommate, Jack had made the mistake of using the front door. Mr Clutterbuck had seen him from his bedroom window, and caught him red-handed.

"Thank goodness we climbed in at the back," sighed Roddy.

Red Card

Jack kept quiet about the real reason for his midnight walkabout, and everyone assumed he was just being his usual rebellious self.

"There's no point in telling everyone the truth," Roddy said to his team-mates when they met again in the team talk room.

"I agree," said Keira. "Humiliating Jack won't make him any nicer to know."

"And if Mr Clutterbuck got to hear about what we were up to last night, we'd all be in trouble," added Marek.

"It's a pity," growled Jimmy. "Everyone would laugh at him and he deserves it for being so horrible."

"But in a way, he did you a favour," said Roddy. "Even though it's not what he intended. After all, you got over your need for the sock last night, didn't you?"

"I hope so," Jimmy sighed. "We'll find out at the next match."

Long Shot

As they broke up to go out to training, Keira hung back to walk with Roddy. "Well done last night," she said in a low voice. "You handled it really well."

Roddy looked at her in surprise. "I only did what anyone would have done," he told her.

"I'm not sure I'd have kept such a cool head," she admitted. "Anyway," she gave him a shy smile. "I just wanted to say that if I was injured or something, I'd choose you as vice-captain any day."

Roddy felt a warm glow inside. "Thanks," he said. Then he sighed. "But Mr Jenkins will never know about last night. I won't get picked for the firsts on leadership qualities like you. I need to concentrate on playing my best football to get noticed."

"We all do," said Keira.

Although Roddy and his friends were tired, there was no opportunity for slacking, and

Red Card

they all had to do their regular morning run.

"What's up with you today?" asked Mr Jenkins as Roddy came in halfway down the field for a change.

"Just didn't sleep too well," Roddy explained.

"You're not the only one," said Mr Jenkins. "What was going on in your house last night?"

Roddy shrugged.

"Well, I hope you'll feel more awake this afternoon," said the coach. "It's coming up to a crucial point in the term. I'm going to be announcing who's in the first team shortly. After your next house match, in fact."

"Really?" Roddy hadn't realised the squad would be named that soon. He felt a quiver of excitement mixed with trepidation. And that wasn't all there was to get excited about. The last house match of the term was coming up, against Stiles.

10. Squad Selection

Heading into the last round of House Cup games for the term, Moore and Charlton were neck and neck on points. The crunch games were the head-to-head Charlton/Moore games to be played by both the second years and the senior girls, but every point from every match would make a difference.

The day of the first years' match against Stiles arrived quickly. Stiles would be without Jack because he'd got a red card from Mr Clutterbuck, and as their captain he'd be a big loss to them. Despite being such a bully, Jack was an excellent footballer.

If Charlton could beat Stiles, they'd have won their first three games in the House Cup.

Squad Selection

Sam had told them not to be complacent against a weakened Stiles team, but Roddy couldn't help feeling relieved about Jack's ban. Jack wasn't even allowed to watch the game – he was doing some schoolwork in the library under Mr Clutterbuck's supervision.

"All right, Jimmy?" Roddy checked before they ran out.

Jimmy gave him a nervous grin. "Hope so," he said.

"Come on, you two," said Keira. "Chin up! With luck, we'll have a walkover today."

Jimmy gulped. "Yeah," he agreed. "With luck."

"Don't be silly, Keira," said Roddy. "Luck's got nothing to do with it!"

Keira clapped her hand to her mouth. "Sorry, Jimmy. Take no notice of me. Come on. Let's get out there!"

Long Shot

The teams are arriving on the pitch now, and it could be tough for Stiles today. They are without their captain Jack Carr, while the Charlton team are still buzzing from their victory against Moore. With first team call-ups around the corner, everyone will be aiming to impress today, so there should be plenty of skills on show. Thirsk, the Stiles vice-captain, shakes hands with Sanders, and tosses the coin. Charlton will kick off the first half.

Dvorski and Perotti start the ball rolling in the centre circle, before passing back to Sanders. Sanders lays it left to Jones, who holds onto it for a while, before setting off down the pitch with the ball at his feet. He passes outside to Eboni Nagel, and surges forward, waiting for the return. He gets it just outside the area, and dummies a pass to Perotti, but keeps going himself. He's one on one with the keeper, and surely this is only going to end one *way. Jones slows his pace, then fires a shot across the goal to nestle in the bottom corner! That's a magnificent run and goal from Jones, and Charlton are ahead in the first minute!*

The Stiles players stood about in shock, as Roddy's team-mates mobbed him.

"Amazing!" screamed Keira. "Simply amazing! You'll get into the first team no problem, playing like that."

Jimmy was yelling praise, too, and looked much happier.

Roddy grinned, and shrugged off the comments. "It's just one goal. We've got the rest of the match to play yet. Come on, the ref wants to restart the game."

After that incredible beginning, Stiles are going to need something equally brilliant to get back into the game. They pass the ball around the midfield for a while, but Mbeki is harassing them, and the Charlton defensive midfielder soon gets in an interception. He feeds the ball to Jones. Could we see another bit of magic from the young Welsh-Brazilian? No, he sees his captain making a run and plays a nice ball, perfect for her to run on to. Sanders takes it in her stride, and hits a searching pass ahead of her, looking for Dvorski. Dvorski flicks the ball on for Perotti, who sees the keeper off his line and tries the lob. Is it dipping fast enough? Yes! It's two for Charlton! The Stiles players look shell shocked.

"Fantastic stuff!" shouted Sam from the touchline. "Keep it up. You've got them on the run. Keep it tight at the back and there'll be no stopping us!"

This Charlton side are showing all the signs of a winning team. They've got lots of attacking flair, and great spirit, too. This could become embarrassing for Stiles; they need to concentrate on damage limitation now.

Squad Selection

The Stiles defence gradually managed to get their act together and, after a couple of scares, they scraped through to half-time without conceding again. The Charlton team were bursting with energy. All they wanted to do was get back out onto the pitch for the second half. Another goal or two could mean vital points at the end of the season.

It's the start of the second half, and Charlton are looking all fired up. But Stiles look like they'd prefer to have stayed in the dressing room. Stiles kicks off, but the team is playing some very negative football. Ashanti Nagel wins the ball in her own half and sets off on a run. Sanders and Jones are offering support, but she's going it alone! She beats one, two, three players down the right wing, before playing it square into the box. Perotti is waiting on the penalty spot to score his second goal of the game, and Charlton's third!

Long Shot

From then on, there was nothing Stiles could do to stop the onslaught. Marek scored a powerful header, and Geno bagged his third goal just before the final whistle. Charlton had won 5–0.

"That's 400 points towards the House Cup!" squealed Sam as they walked off the pitch.

"How do you reckon that?" asked Roddy, who was too tired to add everything up. His legs were aching, and he had a bruise coming on his shoulder from falling heavily after making a tricky tackle.

Keira had the figures in her head. "250 for a win," she explained. "And 25 for each goal, that's 125 to add on."

"Plus we get another 25 for a clean sheet," broke in Jimmy excitedly.

"400 points is a *magnificent* result," said Sam, grinning. "You're going to be Charlton heroes when everyone hears about this!"

Squad Selection

Roddy knew that it wouldn't be so easy when the teams met next term, with Jack on the field, but for now, they could celebrate their win. Hot, muddy and elated, they hurried off to get showered and changed, before a well-deserved tea.

Roddy was so busy chatting to Geno that he almost bumped into Mr Mustard, who was coming the other way round the corner. "Sorry!" said Roddy, afraid he was heading for a telling off, but it didn't come.

Instead, Mr Mustard gave a slight smile. "I saw you on the field this afternoon," he said. "You both did very well."

Once he'd gone, Roddy and Geno looked at each other. "Things really *are* looking up, aren't they?" laughed Roddy.

Mr Jenkins came into the dining hall as Roddy was scoffing his second piece of cake. Word had got around that the first year squad

Long Shot

was going to be announced that evening, so everyone was eager to find out if they'd got a place. Charlton's unbeaten start to the season had given all their players a great chance.

"You'll get in for sure, Roddy," said Keira encouragingly. "You've played brilliantly all term."

Roddy smiled nervously. "You, too. How can they not pick the captain of the team at the top of the table?"

In his own mind, Roddy couldn't help wishing he'd been captain and was now guaranteed a place. It seemed a pity that the leadership qualities Keira had praised him for would remain a secret, but the whole Charlton team were playing so well under Keira he couldn't really begrudge her the position. If they carried on like this, they would win the prize for their year!

"I'm going to name a squad of 23," said

Squad Selection

Mr Jenkins. "Squads are subject to change, so if you're on the list and don't keep up a high enough standard, watch out! There will be plenty of other players lining up to take your place. Equally, if you're not on the list, just keep doing your best in training, and your time will come. Now, without any further ado..."

Roddy's breath quickened. This was it, the moment he'd been waiting for. Did he have what it took to get into the first team? Did the coach think he'd been playing well enough?

"First-year squad." announced Mr Jenkins. "Larsson, Temperley, Bullard, captain will be Sanders..."

Roddy swallowed. How would he bear it if he hadn't made the grade? He tried to concentrate on the list of names, but they were passing in a blur.

Long Shot

"Piper, Dempsey, Thirwell, Dvorski, Walton, Patel, Wilson, Ratcliffe, Nagel A., Nagel E., Carr, Perotti, Jones..."

Jimmy was beaming. He'd made the squad without his sock. Now he certainly didn't need to be superstitious any more.

Roddy looked wildly at Geno. Perotti had been named, he was sure of it, and Geno's happy face confirmed it. But had Roddy heard the next name properly? Had he heard his own name correctly? He imagined so much when he was playing. Was this just another bit of his internal commentary coming to the rescue?

But Geno was nudging him. "Cheer up!" he laughed. "Anyone would think you hadn't got in."

And Jimmy was slapping Roddy on the back. "We did it! We're in the squad! Geno, Marek and us! And Keira's captain."

"Brilliant!" Roddy could see Keira already

out of her seat and walking around the room, congratulating everyone. Roddy was thrilled and relieved. Next term, hopefully, he would be playing against youth sides from some of the best clubs in the country and, maybe one day, his time to be captain would come.

What a lot he would have to talk about when he got home. His parents and Bryn would want to hear all about their matches in the House Cup but, best of all, he'd be able to tell them that he'd made the squad for the first team. He was in! This is what he'd worked for. This is what it was all about. He was at Stadium School, and now he was starting to live his dream.

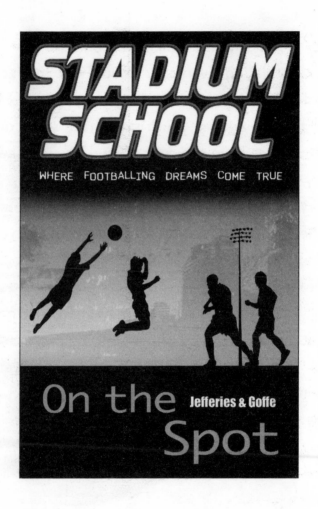

STADIUM SCHOOL

WHERE FOOTBALLING DREAMS COME TRUE

On the Spot

Jefferies & Goffe

Coming December 2008...